CHILDREN'S ROOM
JULIUS FORSTMANN LIBRARY
PASSAIC PUBLIC LIBRARY
195 GREGORY AVENUE
PASSAIC, NEW JERSEY 07055

E772641

J

PASSAIC PUBLIC LIBRARY, NJ

3 2344 05079210 4

D1404690

THE KITE

THE KITE

LUIS GARAY

Tundra Books

CHILDREN'S ROOM
JULIUS FORSTMANN LIBRARY
PASSAIC PUBLIC
195 GR...
PASSAIC, N...

Copyright © 2002 by Luis Garay

Published in Canada by Tundra Books,
481 University Avenue, Toronto, Ontario M5G 2E9

Published in the United States by Tundra Books of Northern New York,
P.O. Box 1030, Plattsburgh, New York 12901

Library of Congress Control Number: 2001095519

All rights reserved. The use of any part of this publication reproduced, transmitted in
any form or by any means, electronic, mechanical, photocopying, recording, or otherwise,
or stored in a retrieval system, without the prior written consent of the publisher – or,
in case of photocopying or other reprographic copying, a licence from the Canadian
Copyright Licensing Agency – is an infringement of the copyright law.

National Library of Canada Cataloguing in Publication Data

Garay, Luis, 1965-
     The kite

ISBN 0-88776-503-3

     I. Title.

PS8563.A598K58 2002   jC813'.54   C2001-903544-6

We acknowledge the support of the Canada Council for the Arts and the Ontario Arts
Council for our publishing program.

We acknowledge the financial support of the Government of Canada through the Book
Publishing Industry Development Program for our publishing activities.

Design: Cindy Elisabeth Reichle

Printed in Hong Kong, China

1 2 3 4 5 6   07 06 05 04 03 02

In Latin America, where I come from, there are thousands of children who live in poverty. I dedicate this book to them, and to the memory of Charles Stothers.

The hard-baked earth by the back door was cool under Francisco's feet, for the sun had not yet risen. He did not mind the early hour. He had often gone with Papa to the marketplace at dawn. They used to have a fruit stall there. Now that Papa was dead, another man arranged the mangoes and plantain, pineapples and oranges, and Francisco sold newspapers on a corner.

"Good-bye, Mama. I'll see you tonight. Be good for Mama, little brother." Francisco patted his mother's belly and made his morning wishes: that he would sell all his papers, that the baby would arrive soon, and that the kite would still be hanging in Señor González's toy stall.

Mama laughed. "Bless you, my boy. Now off you go. Raul will soon be here with the clothes I have to wash."

The sky was growing pink as Francisco made his way along the road. He waved at Señora Martínez.

"How's your mama this morning?" she asked. "Just think, you could be a big brother by tonight!"

Francisco repeated the words "big brother" to himself as he hurried to the newspaper depot.

The other newspaper sellers had gathered by the time Francisco arrived. When his turn came, he held out his arms for his papers. Ten of them. Enough to make a little money, but not so many that he would lose them.

"Here you are, boy. Now, everyone, pay attention. I'll read out today's headlines: Budget cuts! Governor calling for order!"

Francisco tried hard to remember, so that he could call them out to the passersby.

F rancisco made his way into the bustling marketplace. He stopped at Señor González's stall. "Ah, Francisco. Let's see what the world is up to." He cracked his newspaper and settled himself on his stool.

Señor González had the best stall in the whole marketplace. Bright piñatas bobbed from a rod. Balls spilled out of a bucket. There were balloons and dolls and all kinds of toys. But the best, by far, was the kite. It hung from the corner, as if it were ready to fly away. Francisco looked for it every morning.

"Don't worry, boy, it's still there. Why don't you buy it? It is only a few cents. Your mama won't mind."

But Francisco knew that she *would* mind, especially with the new baby coming. He shifted his papers in his arms and turned away.

The marketplace had a rhythm and Francisco was part of it. "Budget cuts! Governor calling for order!" he cried over and over, his voice rising above the sound of transistor radios, a dog's bark, and the *thrum* of a guitar. The vendors called out their wares: pots made of clay, leather bags, bright woven cloth, guitars and ripe fruits and furniture with inlaid designs.

Then, for a moment, it seemed as if everything grew still. A man passed by Francisco, holding his son's hand. The small boy carried a neat package under his arm. Francisco thought of Papa and remembered how he had tried to stay in step with his giant strides whenever they walked together. He squeezed his eyes shut to hold the memory.

By the time he had sold his last paper, the marketplace was almost empty. Francisco sat on a bench, too tired even to eat his orange. He thought about the man with his small son. He remembered his own papa's big laugh, the way he would sing the same funny song over and over, and most of all, how they would go to the big green field and watch the kites rise up in the sky.

His baby brother would never have those sweet memories of Papa. Francisco would be the one to make memories for the baby. The thought of the new baby overwhelmed him, but also cheered him. After all, a new life! Francisco got up and walked home.

The next morning Francisco's newspapers sold quickly. He was making his way to Señor González and the toy stall when Señora Ramírez saw him.

"Would you like to give me a hand, Francisco? Clean up the plantain leaves, will you? There may be a treat for you when you are done."

Francisco gathered up the leaves and the bits of sugarcane that littered the ground around Señora Ramírez's stall. When he was finished, she smiled at him and handed him a fragrant *vigorón*.

"Here you go, Francisco." He knew he should be disappointed. After all, a few extra cents would be welcome at home. But the smell of the fried pork and *cassava* wrapped in a plantain leaf made his mouth water.

Francisco was emptying out the trash from Señora Ramírez's stall at the edge of the marketplace when the boys found him.

"Francisco, it's the baby! You have to go home."

Francisco ran around the outside of the marketplace until he came to the road leading home. The back door was closed. Francisco could not ever remember seeing it shut, and it frightened him. He raced around to the front of the house.

"Mama, Mama! Is everything all right?" He pounded on the door.

"Calm yourself, calm yourself." But it was Señora Martínez's voice, not his mother's, that replied.

"Mama!" he cried.

Finally Señora Martínez opened the door. She winked at him.

"Come to me, my boy." His mother's voice was weak, but full of joy.

"Is this my brother?" Francisco knelt by the bed.

Señora Martínez and Señora Pérez laughed.

"Life is full of surprises, and this is a very nice one. You have a beautiful sister! Her name is Guadalupe," said Señora Martínez. "Now, we've brought you soup and there is a chicken for your supper."

Francisco did not speak. He had seen many babies before, but he had never been a brother before.

The next morning the neighbors came back. This time Señora Martínez brought coffee and *tamales*. Señora Pérez also had a gift: "I am going to do the laundry in place of your mama until she is on her feet."

It seemed impossible to Francisco that he could leave the tiny house and his mother and sister, even for a few hours, but he knew that he had to. It was time to go to work.

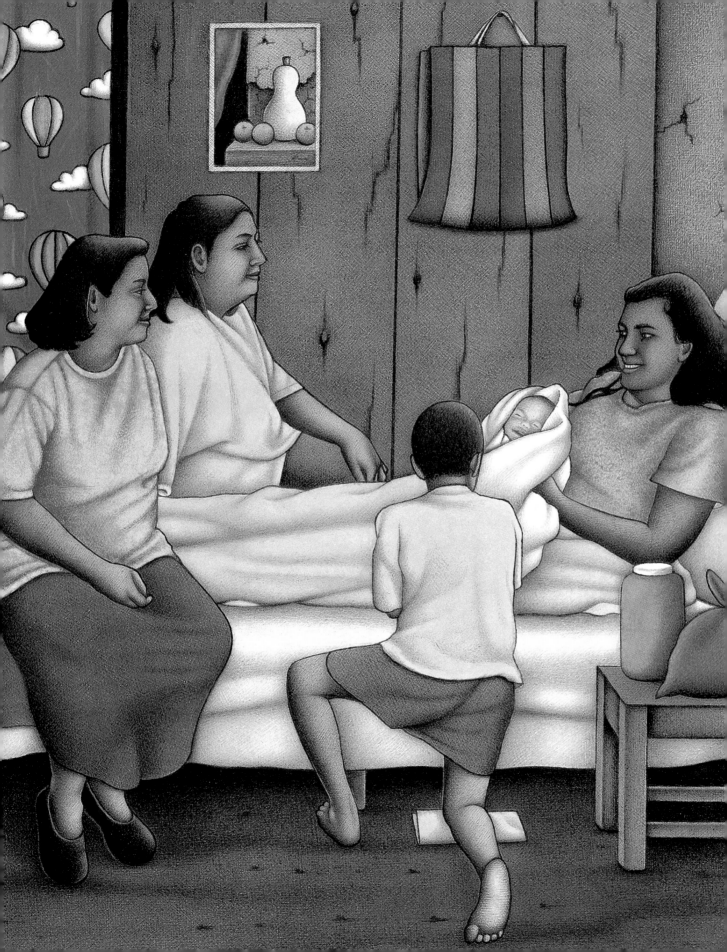

Once he had collected his papers and had the headlines firmly memorized, he hurried to Señor González's stall.

"What's the news today, Francisco?" He reached for a paper.

"It's me who has the news, Señor. I have a new baby sister."

"Ah, that is great news! It calls for a celebration." He untied the kite from the stall, and handed it to Francisco. "When you've finished with your papers, it will be here for you. Señora Ramírez told me how you helped her yesterday, and I know your papa would be proud. Besides, it's not every day you become a big brother."

Francisco beamed. "Gracias, Señor González!"

All the while Francisco cried the headlines, he could not stop smiling. When the papers were finally gone, he took the kite to the field.

At first he could not make it fly, no matter how fast he ran. But then, with one lovely gust, the kite began to rise. It seemed to Francisco that he and the kite and the blue sky and the white clouds were all a chain.

The last time he had been in the field, Papa had been with him. Together they had watched the kites scud across the sky. As the kite tugged his hand, Francisco knew his papa was part of the chain, too.

When he came home, the neighbors had gone. For the first time, he and Guadalupe and Mama were alone.

"Would you like to hold the baby?" asked Mama.

Francisco was nervous as he took the warm bundle. The baby snuggled into his arms.

"Are you happy, my boy?"

Francisco thought of the wishes he had made on this baby before she was born. He knew that some would never come true. Papa would never hug him again, or swing him high into the air. But life is full of surprises. Some are hard to bear.

Others are wonderful.